the OLD WOMAN and HER PIG

AN APPALACHIAN FOLKTALE

retold by **MARGARET READ MACDONALD**

pictures by **JOHN KANZLER**

Pigs for a Penny

HARPERCOLLINS*PUBLISHERS*

Library of Congress Cataloging-in-Publication Data • MacDonald, Margaret Read, 1940— • The old woman and her pig : an Appalachian folktale / retold by Margaret Read MacDonald ; illustrated by John Kanzler.—1st ed. • p. cm. • Summary: Worried that Little Boy will be frightened if she fails to return home before dark, an old woman enlists the aid of some passing animals to coax her new pig across the bridge. • ISBN-10: 0-06-028089-1 (trade bdg.) — ISBN-13: 978-0-06-028089-5 (trade bdg.) • ISBN-10: 0-06-028090-5 (lib. bdg.) — ISBN-13: 978-0-06-028090-1 (lib. bdg.) • [1. Folklore—Appalachian Region. 2. Pigs—Folklore.] I. Kanzler, John, ill. II. Title. • PZ8.1.M159240ld 2006 • 2006000560 • 398.20974'02—dc22 • Designed by Stephanie Bart-Horvath • 1 2 3 4 5 6 7 8 9 10 • ❖ • First Edition

From Granny Mac,
for all her little piglets.
And for all those nights when
the moon does shine
—M.R.M.

To my mother,
a light in the darkness
—J.K.

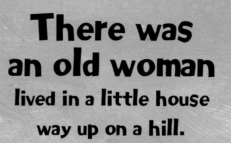

**There was
an old woman**
lived in a little house
way up on a hill.

Had a little boy
that lived with her.
They got along real well,
those two.

One day Little Boy
was playing out in front of the house.
He found a shiny copper penny!

"Ma'am, look what I found!"

"Why, it's a shiny copper penny!
I'll take that right to town
and buy us a fat little pig!

"You stay here and tend the house.
I'll be back before dark
with our piggy."

Off she started
down the road.
She was so happy to be going
to town to buy a pig.
She started singing.
"Goin' to town,
gonna buy a little pig.
Jig jog jig jog jiggety-jig!"

Came to a bridge.
Started crossing that bridge,
dancing a jig.
"Goin' to town,
gonna buy a little pig.
Jig jog jig jog jiggety-jig!"

Back on the road again,
she was still singing.
"Goin' to town, gonna buy a little pig.
Jig jog jig jog jiggety-jig!"

Came to the marketplace.

"Mr. Pig Farmer, here's a shiny copper penny.
I'd like to buy a fat little pig."

"A shiny copper penny!
I'll take your shiny copper penny.
Pick out any pig you want."

She looked around.
Picked out the fattest little pig of all.
"I'll take **THAT** one."

She was so happy
to be going home
with that little pig.
"Went to town
and I bought a little pig.
Jig jog jig jog jiggety-jig!"

Little Pig was happy
to be going home
with that old woman.
He ran along behind her
just squealing.
"Oink oink oink oink,
oink oink oink!
Oink oink oink oink,
oink oink oink!"

Came to the bridge.

Old Woman started crossing that bridge.
"Went to town and I bought a little pig.
Jig jog jig jog jiggety-jig!"

Little Pig started right after her.

"Oink oink oink oink
EEEEEE!!!"

That little pig

would not set one foot
on that bridge.
He was scared of the water.
He was scared of the height.
He just stood there and
squealed.

Old Woman

came back.
She pulled that pig.
She pushed that pig.
That pig would not move.

Old Woman began to worry.

It was starting to get dark.
Her little boy was at home all by himself.
He might get scared.

Then she saw the moon coming up.
The moon would give Little Boy light,
so maybe he wouldn't be so scared.

Old Woman sat down

and began to cry.
She sang a sad little song to herself.
"I can't get to my little boy tonight.
It's almost dark . . .
but the moon does shine."

Just then, along came a dog.
Old Woman thought he might help.
"Dog, dog, would you bark at pig?
Pig won't cross the bridge,
and I can't get home to my little boy tonight."

"Nope," said the dog.
"I won't do it."

"Well, that's not nice."
And the old woman
began to cry.
"I can't get to my little boy tonight.
It's almost dark . . .
but the moon does shine."

Old Woman saw a rat running by.

"Rat, rat, would you nip dog?
If you would nip dog,
dog would bark at pig,
pig would cross the bridge,
and I could get home
to my little boy tonight."

"**Nope**," said the rat.
"**I won't do it.**"

"Well, that's not nice."
And the old woman began to cry.
"I can't get to my little boy tonight.
It's almost dark . . .
but the moon does shine."

Just then a cat came by.

"Cat, cat, would you worry rat?
Then rat will nip dog,
dog will bark at pig,
pig will cross the bridge,
and I'll get home
to my little boy tonight."

The cat said, "Little boy? Little boy?
Is that the same little boy
who used to stroke my fur?"

"That's the same little boy."

"Is that the same little boy
who used to give me a saucer of cream?"

"Same little boy."

"Is that the same little boy who used to scratch
behind my ears and it felt so GOOD?"

"That's the SAME little boy!"

"Then
OF COURSE
I'll help!"
said the cat.

The dog began to bark at the pig.

"WOOF! WOOF! WOOF!"

And the little pig
ran over the bridge
and up the road home . . .
just squealing.

"EEEEEEEEEEEE......"

That old woman
ran right along
behind him.
"Went to town
and I bought a little pig.

Jig jog
jig jog
jiggety-
jig!"

When she got home, she **HUGGED** that little boy. And you know, he hadn't been afraid at all because . . .

"It sure was dark . . .
but the moon
did shine."

AUTHOR NOTE

The traditional story of "The Old Woman and Her Pig" (Tale Type 2030, Motif Z41) appeared in print as early as 1842 in James Orchard Halliwell-Phillipps's THE NURSERY RHYMES OF ENGLAND (London: T. Richards), and it has appeared in countless versions since. This retelling is inspired by a Kentucky variant collected by folklorist Leonard Roberts in SANG BRANCH SETTLERS (Pikeville College Press, 1980). The crying song and the little boy appear in Roberts's version. The jogging song and the helpful cat are my inventions.

"CRYING SONG"

I can't get to my lit-tle boy to-ni-ght. It's al-most dark but the moon does shine.

"JOGGING SONG"

Goin' to town gon-na buy a lit-tle pig. Jig jog jig jog jig-ge-ty jig!